# NONNA'S STORIES - II

## SECOND IN THE SERIES

## TERESA DI SCLAFANI DE NASCA

# CONTENTS

**Nonna's Stories - II**

Second in the series

Published by TecnoTur Publishing

Layout by Allan Tépper

ISBN of the paperback version:

979-8-9988687-5-7

ISBN of the electronic version (*ebook*):

979-8-9988687-6-4

*I dedicate this work to:*

*- My son, Professor Carlos Sayas Torres, who was born of a miracle. A hug and kiss from your mother who loves you so much.*

*- My sons Toni and Enzo.*

*- My three grandchildren, Salvatore Jesús, Enzito and Salvatore Antonio. Kisses to all.*

# EDITOR'S NOTE
# ON THE WORD «NONNA»

The Italian word *Nonna* in English means Grandmother.

**1**

## ALIA AND ITS TRADITIONS

The school in the village of Alia had up to fifth grade. There was the San Giuseppe school, which was for girls, and the agency school, which was for boys. At that time, the teacher was good and in first grade we were taught division and two-digit multiplication. Maestro Malacuso was my brother's teacher in the third grade.

One day a week they were taken to work in the fields. If there were children who were taught, they were punished behind the blackboard and hit with a reed in the hand. The children of poor farmers could not study. It was the children of the middle class and the rich who studied. Today there are many graduates from any village.

At that time wheat had a very low price, since the United States had a lot of production. What was leftover was burned. People started to emigrate. They were looking for industries and it was all in northern Italy. Women didn't study, they had to wash and iron, they had to do housework, make food for the men farmers.

For enjoyment of the small society, there was a local burst for the middle class: there were those who played cards for money and others who played just for fun. The great society served for parties. The good wife saved and was the one who sold wheat to buy clothes in the month of May.

There were those who sold it to buy things for whims. If it remained without grain and remained lending grains. When it was tomato season, the sauce and the extract were made, which was put with boards in the sun. Olive oil was made and the olives were kept to be eaten in the winter. Wine was drunk all year round and Sicilian wine was 25 to 30 degrees. The production of almonds, fruits and vegetables was abundant and jam was made. Chickens were raised and eggs were laid in the house. The tree was pruned to make firewood, which was used for the stove and oven, there was no electric stove. The wood was used to make furniture and cabinets.

Christmas, Carnival and New Year were parties of dancing and eating. The tradition of the feast was the *tarantella* and the *contradanza*. They were those masters who called for San Giuseppe, who made sweet bread, sphinx and canola. That was the Sicilian custom, but it no longer exists anywhere. They made the baby Jesus, the Madonna, St. Joseph and 12 children. Everything was made to eat and the Apostles attended. Many friends did it by promise.

My little sister was operated on for appendicitis when she was 8 years old and she has a photograph as a souvenir. My father made that promise. The feast of the Madonna, with music, movies and processions, where there were several promises. New dresses and booties were bought. Holy Week was the mortuary and the life of Jesus Christ and the apostles. September 4 was the day of Santa Rosalía and there were movies, singers and music. October 20 was the day of the Sorrowful Mother. This was the custom of my town, Alia.

In the month of June was the grain harvest. A large round area was made and with two mules the farmer would turn around. They put a handkerchief on their heads and hair and called them the Madonnas of Gibilmana. They kept the body and soul and many other things. Those who made the feast passed by and they were given grains. The feast was not done by the mayor's office, it was done by the farmers. The harvest was sold. In the future, the straw that remained of the grain was separated and given to the animals. This was the custom, sacrifice to bring a piece of bread to the house, the hens, eggs and chicken went to the house in the field.

The young people got married with big parties. The parents gave them the house and collaborated with furniture and tablecloths. This was done by those who had land and cattle. Dad married and had five girls and two boys. There was no honeymoon.

When the party was over, they would leave, crouch on the balcony to hear the serenade and all the guests would accompany them to the house. When a young lady got married in the morning, for eight days they brought her food, once the mother and once the mother-in-law. For women, at that time there was a lot of work, because there was no water or plumbing. The water accumulated, she put it in the pitcher and went to throw it away. Pigs were raised and slaughtered in October. That was used to make sausage and with the fat and lard.

We girls played uncles *Pigú*: ten squares, five on one side and five on the other side, skipped. They played Aunt Mase, with four wires that pulls and encourages. The children played *strumula* and arrived home with their pants without buttons. Today they play differently, with telephones and computers. What money was to be spent? They were men and women who married and formed a family with children. Today marriage is serious, there are many divorces and they don't want children. They used to have very nice houses with gardens.

The war of Greece and the Romans, the great conflict in 1914 and 1918, the Soviet Union, the fall of the Berlin Wall, the end of the Soviet Union, the mafiosi capable of kidnapping and killing. Mafia security emerged in Sicily, Sardinia, Calabria, the countryside, Tuscany, Lombardy, Piedmont. With knowledge of the past, the citizens of Alia and Corleone did not know the history of Sicily, the Spaniards and the Prince of Bourbon. In 1812 we were a free city, not subject to the feudal citizen of Palermo, the oldest. Rome, Athens, Naples and the history of the citizen of Palermo.

Horacio Cangilla, in 1860 Palermo was the capital of Sicily, the golden shell. Petralia, San Matteo Palermitano, legitimized. Seen the history of illiterate Italy, Eugenio Guccione's knowledge of the history of the country. The book of Liborio Guccione who as a child had walked in Tuscany. The resistance group Carbagnama Lucca, Easy Editors, 1978. Dispersed Boggiborzi Editors, 1984. Missions Rosa Balilla, resistance aliceti of Milano, Evangelista Editores, 1987, Carbagnama Resistance.

I have read the whole story with Eugenio Guccione. I knew him as a child and when he was five years old he would get up on a chair and say I am the lawyer Eugenio Guccione. He had a passion to be a lawyer since he was a child. Liborio Guccione had finished the book and said that women dressed like uncontrolled Arabs. When he saw this book, he sent a photograph to Father Antonino Vicari and to the trustee. Guccione was 18 years old in 1958.

My grandmother was born in 1890 and died in 1972. She wore *paltó*, half heels and a veil. We did not talk about my aunt Ana, who was my grandmother's sister and always wore a hat, bag and gloves. My grandfather was born in 1880 and died in 1964. When I said «upstairs,» my sister-in-law Ana had to leave the table.

Pietro Tomasso and son Giovanni, 1461, passed the possessions to Reinaldo Crespo in 1514 in favor of the son of Federico, in possession of the same family. Federico Crespo sold the village of Alia to Vincenzo Imparbara for the sum of eleven. 1239 23 1011. He reserved the right for his heir Vincenzo Imparbara with Eleonora Crispi. Of Federico with union of Baron Pietro and three women, Laura Ballisera Biondoligi. After the death of the husband, Eleonora with the very young son, Pietro, inherited on May 7, 1537. He kept the fund and those who lived in this fief with the wife. They were treated as slaves, they and the children who knew nothing of life.

Alia is built on a mountain and has a cemetery where the dead were thrown like dogs in a hole that was there. It was called at that time the old cemetery. The town of Alia had four churches. The Mother Church next to the Palazzo del Cavaliere had a clock that woke up all the workers in the early morning. The small Church of San Giuseppe. The Church of St. Anne is quite large with the tiered staircase over the staircase, I remember that Salvatore Nasca, my husband, had left before he went to Venezuela. He was young and strong, he was 16 years old and he did everything with enthusiasm. The Church of Santa Rosalía is at the entrance of the village.

With the Second World War, this village almost disappeared, because the cannons were placed high. If they were left, the village of Alia would disappear. A general said he was in charge. The Mother of Grace saved this town.

My father belonged to the Madonna of San Giuseppe and the Holy Trinity. There are private cemeteries and if he paid he could keep them for 30 years, insured with the niches. From then on, dad has been 30 years. When he was taken out, he was perfect and after years in the ground he had remained. The bones are now in a small shed and my mother is in the niches. I hope the private grave will remain, if you pay every year and if you put the light on. That is the great history of the village of Alia, which has received so much affection.

When my son was one year old, 57 years ago, a miracle was performed on me by the saintly Blessed José Gregorio Hernández. He died in the middle of the night and after half an hour he came back to life. I was 27 years old. I made the saint in the town of Alia, inaugurated on June 18, 2023. It is in the Church of Santa Rosalía, at the entrance of the village.

2

# HISTORY OF AN INJUSTICE

The only breadwinner in life, he lives on alms. Vincenzo is in the Ancona prison. The worker was waiting at the exit of the prison. Di Salvo Francesco, thanks to justice, the Ministry of grace and the delegate, P.S. Marasciallo, R.R. police and the praetor sent after knowing and fell. The brothers of Heaven only help and blessings.

Alia, November 29, 1901. Leone Cardinale accuses and excuses him for a miscarriage of justice. The poor innocent man meets the murderer in silence. Nobody talks to the public safety authority, the strongest police force. Di Marco has lost a lot of blood. Angelo Moso is already tired of what Di Marco will say. With much blood loss, Di Marco will not see brother Drago and will not recognize anyone. The two families are destroyed. Only the authority will recognize the blood of the rooster. He had killed a rooster and was waiting for the son coming from Montemaggiore. The authorities have declared that the blood was human.

On August 1, 1872, the old murdered Antonina Di Salvo, seeing Di Marco. The grandson Drago is presented with another file to the prosecutor's office of Termine. The transfer to the procurator's office of Palermo, another file, of Termine and Palermo. Professor Ciro Leoni Cardinale, young, intelligent and noble-hearted man, found a flaw in the long article of the newspaper Il Sole, the proof of the citizen of Alia in defense of the unhappy, so much that he announces the freedom and the honor in sight and four innocent brothers.

On August 20, 1873 the court of Assisi, Palermo, publicly condemns the accused to death and imprisonment. The lions continue. According to the Superior Court of Contention, Augustine is guilty. On May 12, 1874, Brother Damiano Drago, who lived in Montemaggiore, was on the scaffold. He was excluded after a year, died of heartbreak, leaving his wife and son orphaned. Antonino Drago, sentenced to 30 years, had paid the penalty. The mother, deprived of her son after 30 years, leaves with her eyes lowered. The other dies in prison. Francesco Di Salvo, 53 years old, goes home to his poor house. The whole Drago family is beaten. In 1873, Agostino, Vincenzo and Rosalino receive the maximum sentence of 30 years and Antonino 19 years.

On August 1, 1872 had changed to the low territories of Di Sclafani, owner Princess Cordova Di Marco and grandson appear in Alia. Di Marco and Drago, the police, the lieutenant, RR. CC. for finding the knife with which he had killed the rooster. He shouted: «Eureka! They are brilliant». Di Salvo was brought to a dark room and with his eyes on the wall he said «I am innocent». He had a dead face, it was impossible to speak. Rosalino, Antonino and Agustino were left in the prison of Alia, after 4 days in the prison of Palermo.

In September 1873, given at the Assisi Court of Palermo presided over by the gentleman Guccione, citizen in the Drago trial. Di Salvo had no money. Declares Agostino Drago, Di Sally, Lorci, Santa Flavia, resident in Bagheria Visida Cardosi. The Ministry of Grace was refuted, it is refuted after 13 years and 3 months. He had been in the most painful of the old city and was brought to Ancona by the prison warden, Di Luca.

The director Vincenzo Mardaceo tells him that grace did not accept him and on August 28 he opens the prison door. In Sicily there were always mistakes. Vincenzo Drago was skinny, after 30 years, and in the family a grandson of Drago Gennaio. In 1902 the prosecutor's office of Termine sent him to the prosecutor's office of Palermo, where they found evidence. Drago and Di Salvo were in a hostel, Elena in Piazza Stazione, accompanied by citizens of Palermo and Alia, colleagues who came from Florence.

Drago Vincenzo was short statured. He had a broad forehead and small eyes. Six years he has talked with a priest of the village where he was born. Rosalino Drago, 60 years old, after serving the sentence in the file will be to see the newspaper Il Sole, N 314, fine 329, year 1- 41- 67- 218. On July 13, 1902, the prosecutor of the court of Termine in Alia makes a very rigorous minute.

Brother Augustine was beheaded in Palermo on May 12, 1874 and Brother Antonio died of fright. In gazette on July 19, 1881, Damiano, of the dead mother of sorrow, Montemaggiore Belsito. They are unfortunate and are not forgotten. Alia, August 25, 1903, return of a sister of Drago. Newspaper of Sicily, September 2, 1903 the Leoni gang. Innocence has become a committee of the most honest people. Grace, 30 years deprived of freedom. April 5 and August 28, 30 years of martyrdom.

Vincenzo with half a year in freedom, a postcard of Naples arrives in Palermo to meet his grandson. Apparently Leone, Giocchino, Solito, Cotone, any Aliese èrspm residing in America, porrazo and pagan is in the penal toilet. The murderer Agostino Drago, the father Franchi who attended the error of that ministry, Tassardelli. 30 years, being innocent.

On August 27, 1903 a telegram arrives from Rome to free the prisoners of Ancona, Drago Vincenzo Luciano. Alia reports 231 errors to the newspaper, which always speaks of justice. In 1872 the conditions were tragic. Di Marco Rosalía, the grandson Cosimo and people of the family. The sentence of the court of Assisi of Palermo, on August 23, 1873, the brothers Agostino, Antonino, Vincenzo and Rosalino Drago, Luciano the farmer, Di Salvo Francesco, Paulo, are released with sovereign grace. Very late recognition that they were innocent, but they are alive.

Dreffur in France, songbook of Dentaro, the Saputo brothers, di Paulino, Nizzola, unfortunate of Italy and France. The devil's island, the Renne court with courage to free him. In Italy, the songbook restored to the family of the unfortunate of Santo Paulo, Mauro Castel Verde, requires grace. The last Di Marco to the year was found agonizing and it remained to di Marco if he knew him. He had a hole in his throat and his head was down. They understood that he was guilty and that the chicken blood was human. No one has reviewed the court of Assisi and Palermo on August 29, 1873.

He was executed on May 12, 1874 in a prison in Palermo, his eyes filled with tears. Tired of praying in that small cell of the scaffold, with a dark lamp and his eyes to heaven. «My God, have mercy on my mother,» he would say, thinking of his poor mother. Corruption, the First World War and a court in a small town of Alia. What will it be in all of Sicily?

On July 31 and August 1, 1872, a poor old woman of 80 years of age was approached and tried alive. The neighbors put out the fire. The grandson Di Marco lived with the grandmother to keep her company. The corpse was on the bed and they had made the hole when the relatives arrived. When the authorities arrived, no neighbor had spoken, there was fear. The Drago brothers were accused and the authorities arrested them for having found the chicken's blood and the bloody fork. I was waiting for my son to arrive from Montemaggiore and he was coming back from work. Justice has not done any blood test. They were working the land and the cows, the grandson knew nothing.

# 3

## ALIA'S PEOPLE

Father Pelta preached the mass and Father Guccione said the silent mass, which many liked because it was short. There was the shoemaker, the deaf carpenter, the blacksmith and the apothecary. There was a ministry of agriculture that set the prices. There were few Carabinieri left with miserable facilities and they came from Montecatini. The first was Gialombardo and Todaro, representatives of Montecatini.

There was little agriculture and farmers to harvest the olives, almonds and walnuts. The harvest was poor because of the snow, it was always raining and it was very hot, with storms in the north. Bonfires were built for the wood stove and the kitchen. On Sundays any rabbit or chicken was roasted and also for Christmas and New Year's Eve. New dresses and shoes were put on the hook, with a bow on the sleeve. Two pieces of candy at Christmas and two pieces of coal were put in. Everyone waited for Aunt María, who had a basket in one hand and a towel in the other.

Vincenzo Guccione bought a machine and went to Michelle Concettina. We walked in the well Raciura, land of my father and Uncle Atiliano. There was the square of Giuseppe Verdi, Leonardo Da Vinci street, Pupi's opera. The countess puppet sang: «I am frozen, furious». From Jerusalem, Orlando, Ronaldo and Angélica. The children know the Sicilian history. Giuseppe Garibaldi of 1860, slept one night in the village of Alia, Garden City.

We were on the bus and suddenly it stopped, we had arrived at Paloma rock while the train was arriving. To go to the capital on the train you could see the whole village, the trees, the sea. We slept on the train La Vittorina. The Guccione Palace belonging to the Guccione gentleman in the Santa Rosalía neighborhood, next to the mother church. The fields of Termine and Palermo, different landscapes from the village of Alia. Father Pelta spoke that he has only forbidden me the walk of the school with the teacher the Gualla.

In the regime of the time in Termine Merese, the militia commanded. They brought tears to my eyes and the villagers like Giochino Martino and Giochino Argono. Cut and sew, to Estefano and Eugenio, aunt Rosina, Estefano's mom. Close the door. We walked in the square of St. Joseph, the area of St. Anne, the entrance of Montemaggiore, the church of St. Joseph, the church of St. Rosalía that crosses. It is celebrated in the casino with guitar, violin and philharmonic. Miser Alia, on Sundays and the whole church.

The bus known from broken master, Paloma rock service, has improved the service with the intervention of Mattiucci. Next to the motorcycle with carriage, the means of transport of that time, the mule, the donkey, the train La Vittorina, the Ferrari of Don Vincenzo. On that street there were motorcycles and scooters. Pietro Runfo, a lawyer of that time, bought a Guzzi motorcycle. We used to go to Santa Rosalía square with the Sicilian uncle, where there was the book by <u>Garbagnaba</u>, the only Sicilian writer I personally read.

Don Roberto Pirandello, Roma, Lampedusa, Sciacca, Milano. Publisher Vangelista 1973. Francesco Renda, memory of the farmer August 29, 1973. Palermo 1945 - 1946. Translated in Milan in 1976. Palermo 1947, making exchange after the postwar period. Fascism in trouble, 1943. Portella della Ginestra, May 1, 1947. Francesco Renda accompanied this book that he writes in 1976.

## 4

# THE MEMORY OF ALIA, SICILY

It was a mule and horse shoe made by Salvatore Nasca. He had the technique for horseshoeing and forging of that time, but he did not use the forge. There was no welder. He heated the iron and carried it with the mallets.

The things he made were welded over time, folding boxes. Everything that was related to working with iron. He has made a boat and everything that was iron craftsmanship.

Salvatore Nasca died 15 years and 6 months ago. I remember what Teresa Di Sclafani de Nasca, her children and grandchildren do.

5

# TERESA DI SCLAFANI

I know the history of Alia well. I was born there on February 16, 1940. Most of these characters I have met. The only ones I have not met are the Drago brothers and their injustice. I knew Father Guccione and the mutual mass, the injustice to the working class, the rich man who one day took over the land and gave it to contract. I met the Guccione gentlemen, Giovanni Don Vincenzo and Giochino and their sons. They are martyrs of what the grandfather has done. The mafioso gentleman was doing well without sweating the loss, since they were rich. That gentleman Guccione became rich with smuggling and the Mafia.

A woman who was a palm reader passed by. He was sitting on a bench and said to her: «You will be rich. Your children will have to mortgage everything. Your grandchildren will be poor and will have to study and work.» Today the memory of those will be measured in the sweat of many innocent people and put many innocent people in jail. May God protect their heirs.

**6**

# MY GREAT-GRANDFATHER LUCIO ORFANELLO

He was studying to be a priest and was going to be ordained, but he didn't continue. According to my mother, grandfather used to tell them to go to mass and to the sacristy. He married Agata Lopresti and they had four daughters and two sons, one of whom died. He worked for 40 years in the post office, telegraph and bank. It was war time, the First World War. When the telegram arrived, he took it to the families in the evening.

He died 83 years ago and I was his great-granddaughter. He did not walk. After he died, I went to visit his daughter Ignacia, to say goodbye in the United States. He was a saint.

7

# JOSELITO IS ON HIS WAY

It was a very happy marriage waiting for the stork. Finally Joselito arrived as we expected, a little angel, growing up very well. The first steps, the first word mom, the second word dad. Arriving at high school, then first grade, finishing elementary and middle school. As the father passes all grades exempted and Joselito is very intelligent. The father says he looks like him, the mother says he looks like her. He looks like both of them.

Joselito starts college and is exempted when unfortunately his father dies of a heart attack. Joselito was thinking of becoming an internist, but changed to a cardiologist-surgeon. His mother was worried but Joselito decided his path. As a surgeon, the best thing to do was to save lives. That was his thing. Now came the hardest part, getting married. He marries a young woman who studied with him, who has a 15 year old daughter. She is very happy and travels with her mother in Europe. As they did not know each other, he divorced, leaving the mother and daughter to support each other. She lost the divorce.

He marries a second time with a good woman, doctor. He has a daughter, a good student who is exempt. He appears in several magazines. Eventually he becomes an internist and starts working as a cardiologist in a hospital with many patients. He arrives tired at night. In the United States they do not consult as in other countries, they only feel the heartbeat. After having all the family problems, he dedicates himself to saving lives. Joselito is not interested in money, he is interested in saving lives.

He has a good position and does speaking engagements. He earns a lot of money, but he was a little uncomfortable with the supervision. A lady knows the environment and writes to the governor as a political flag, to set up a clinic and a hospital for the poor. A friend tells her «let's become independent». He accepted, but something he had not thought of happened: all the cardiologists left the hospital, something that Joselito had not foreseen. The hospital made him another proposal, improving his salary with much more work.

He decides not to leave. The lady tells him to go out, but Joselito always answers «I'm fine». His mother is happy with everything Joselito does. If his father were alive, he would tell him «come out, it's not right here». A psychic tells him, looking into his eyes, that there is a picture with a carved frame and a name underneath. Joselito stares at her.

He does not want to make the daughter known and is very jealous. He invites to a dinner to make his family known. The grandmother is a fake, the grandmother of fairy tales. He is happy and forgets that he is a great cardiologist. In the distant future, he will do a transplant. Joselito has an offer to go to a hospital complex with 4 to 16 floors. What luck! He doesn't want to take advantage of it.

After his mother, there is his false grandmother who loves him. He does not try to win and in the end it will be the grandmother who had a long life expectancy, 84 years. He lived through the war, the happiness of work is ten percent, ninety percent is the good we do for others. That is true happiness. It is not money, money is a means to live. Don't forget that, Joselito. I love you.

Your grandmother.

8

# FIORELLA

This work had to be carried out daily by crews that took turns on a regular basis. Another group took on the task of washing the floors. The chosen ones had to carry heavy buckets of water from the distant spring and undertake the cleaning. The person who refused, either for good reason or because of any physical impediment, was punished with 30 lashes. Some unhappy old or sick person succumbed to the rigor of the inhuman treatment. When this happened, the order was to throw the victim's body in the same crater, the recipient of misfortune. They were in charge of carrying out the sad task. Neither a prayer nor a cross over that man sacrificed as an offering to the homeland outraged by so much cruelty, loved and poorly fed alike.

While all this was going on, in the village there on the slopes of Silveri Castle, the group of recruits destined to perform the most degrading tasks. The Nazis were pork consumers.

They had installed at the foot of the walls of the Castle several pigsties and in them they raised every animal stolen from the peasants of the area, also taking advantage of the proximity of a spring of fresh water that gushed in the middle of the neighboring forest.

The obligation of maintaining one of the pigsties fell on the group of men from Terracotta. They were compelled to collect animal excrement by hand, place it in a wooden crate, carry it to the nearby forest and finally throw it into a huge crater opened by a bomb.

«I'll go to the good, in an emergency,» he said, «and you know what you are doing». The siege of Terracotta continued and its inhabitants continued to be victims of harassment and abuse. With repressed rage, they watched as helpless objects as the Nazis seized the few groceries left in the stores, looting and confiscation of goods were the order of the day.

Anyone who dared to protest was executed in the public square. Mothers and marriageable daughters were forced to confront those madmen, who were accustomed to swallowing abundant wine, became irrational beasts and did not listen to pleas or cries, carrying out the most abominable acts of violence and rape. The food consisted of a daily carrot soup, cold and tasteless, lacking any vitamin substance. During the winter the situation became worse.

«Don Genaro, yes, it is I, Simón Tancredi, who helps the one who despises you so much. You only intended to take a paw on the ground away from your daughter Fiorella».

«My child,» Sacropanti stammers as her eyes filled with tears. «She's left alone, helpless - where will she be now?»

«Father Perpetual Father guides you, be reassured. He has you hidden in his church and protects you».

«Arbert, Arbert,» shouted the guard on duty when he caught the two conversing.

Approaching them with a feline leap, he crossed several times with the whip the face of Genaro Sacripanti, who, unprepared for the brutal attack, fell to the ground bleeding profusely. Simone did not hesitate to help him, receiving several kicks in the stomach, but she did not desist in her attempt to help the fallen man.

«Shit,» muttered the Nazi, walking away instantly. Simone carrying the wounded man to bed, carried him to the barrack and laid him on his cot. The wretch then asks between sobs «What are you doing, this is for her, isn't it?»

«I do it for that too, but you are a human being and deserve to be cared for.»

«Boy, boy, boy, all is forgotten. When Fiorella finds out she'll be proud of you. We'll get out of this hell alive someday.»

The reference by Destripado increased the Nazi lieutenant's eagerness to possess the young Fiorella. «Beware of lying,» says Müller facing the informer. «If you cheat me, to the wall.»

«Gutted never lies.»

«Speak up at once, where is he hiding?»

«In the church of San Rafael. Father Perpetuo hides them in the sacristy.»

«Take me there, I don't want to waste time.»

«Sorry Lieutenant, I can't oblige.»

«What do you say?»

«I would give myself away to my own kind, do you understand?»

«Yes, of course. You're a vile coward, just like all your countrymen,» Müller replied in a contemptuous tone. «Get out of my sight already, you animal.»

Immediately he called the two escorts and with them, aboard a Mercedes Benz convertible, he went to the place indicated by the spy. It was getting dark, in the silence of the sacristy, Father Perpetuo, breviary in hand, was preparing to say the last prayer of the day. With slow steps, from one side of the small room to the other, the faint glow of a candle implored the Most High to put an end to so many outrages. Fiorella is still awake.

«Father, when Vitolo finishes the prayers I will sleep.»

«For the record, it wasn't me forcing you to come back.»

«Don't worry Father, I had no choice. Remigia's house was destroyed by the bomb and she died in the incident...»

The dialogue was abruptly interrupted by the screech of a braking noise, a garbled caller approaching from the adjacent street. Instinctively, the friar urged the young woman to remain still. He went to open the door of the sacristy to see what was happening. In doing so, he almost bumped into Lieutenant Müller. A sudden panic seized the religious. However, appearing calm, he asked dismissively, «To what do I owe such an unexpected visit?»

«No hypocrisy, friar,» exclaimed the S.S. officer in an aggressive tone, «Is she in?»

«She who?»

«Don't act surprised, don't lie». He accompanied the admonition with a strong push that made the friar stagger and he entered the sacristy. He scrutinized every nook and cranny, checking everything meticulously.

«Tell the truth if you don't want to regret it. I know you have her hidden here.»

«Whom are you looking for?»

«Fiorella Sacripanti, you old jerk.»

«Ah, it's about her. She was here until yesterday and left early this morning, I think to the house of an aunt of hers, the Baroness Adelaida Balzi, there in the town of Caldarrosa.»

Fiorella from her hiding place did not miss a word of the conversations. She was on the point of giving herself up, but Father Perpetual continued to deny the lieutenant. Considering himself mocked, he put his hand to his whip and crossed the friar's face several times. Blood spurted on his face, a mirror of meekness, staining his venerable face.

«When will this nightmare end?»

«Nobody knows in war.»

They conversed in low voices, at the beginning of the long lawn that marks the boundary between Sacripanti's possessions and the path that leads to Simón Tancredi's humble dwelling. Witness of the laconic and anguished dialogue, the mute on the banks of the Erbio River, which with its leafy shade gave shelter to the young couple during the summer afternoon. Only one person knows that idyll, the old Capuchin friar, parish priest of the church of St. Raphael, patron saint of the village of Terracotta. A religious respected and loved by all the inhabitants for his kindness and official-dom, always ready to help the flock in need.

His worldly name was Plinio Baldassarri and his religious name was Padre Perpetuo. He facilitated the meetings of young people by welcoming them in the sacristy, a safe place where no one dared to discover them. He justified the singular behavior stimulated by the proven animosity and contempt that the arrogant Genaro Sacripanti, father of the young woman, felt towards Simone Tancredi. For the arro-gant landowner, no one, least of all his employees, no matter how honest and cultured they were, was worthy of looking up to his only daughter.

«Be brief, you are in the house of the Lord,» he asked, closing the door behind him. He left the place and knelt down in front of the miraculous crucifix of <u>Numana</u>, pondering and almost wanting to justify his behavior, he murmured to the mute interlocutor paraphrasing St. Augustine: «Love and do what you want».

The inhabitants of the village of Terracotta during the afternoon of that distant September 8, 1943, learned through the radio of the armistice between General Pietro Badoglio, commander and chief of the Italian army, and the chief of the Allied Command, whose troops had landed in Sicily occupying part of the island. By such a decision, the Italian peninsula was cut into two parts: the southern end in the hands of the Allies and the northern center under the German boots. The latter, considering themselves betrayed because of the armistice signed by Badoglio, from that date on would commit the most vile reprisals, the most inhuman outrages against the entire civilian population.

For the Nazis, the Italians of traitors would henceforth be deserving of all kinds of retaliation and revenge and had to be crushed like insects. In a short time, their barbarism, with the help of the Fascist militia composed of stateless Italians, reached all social sectors. No institution, no matter how noble and humanitarian, would escape the abuses of the horde.

On the edge of one of the most important roads leading to the capital of Rome, a battalion of the so-called S.S., led by Lieutenant Müller, a favorite pupil of the physician Joseph Mengele, sadly nicknamed «the angel of death», took possession of the town's municipal palace, an architectural jewel of the Baroque period. This hitherto respected property was the object of obscene changes with the ensuing period. Huge posters with the figure of the Führer were kept there and enormous swastikas covered all its exterior walls.

The flags of the Third Reich displaced the historical facts of the independence of the Italian nation. They went to the flames their libraries, burned all the books belonging to writers pride of Italian literature. The venerable retired language teacher, on the occasion with the first authority of the city council Jacobo Milzi, upon witnessing the intolerable abuses, dared to raise his voice in protest. He was pushed out of the place and thrown down the steps.

More patriotic and faithful employees abandoned their posts, fleeing in terror. In a few days the terror took hold, and within a week of the arrival of the S.S., the first conscription took place one afternoon. Young and old, single and married, rich and poor, were taken from their respective homes and forced into trucks. They violently broke into each home, beating and beating their way in, knocking down every obstacle in their path, mocking and making fun of their dwellers.

The aggrieved housewives, who tried to placate those fierce beasts with supplications, did not succeed in pleading. Simone Tancredi's *nonna* realized that her only grandson was being dragged to the recruit's truck and wanted to avoid it. The intelligent old woman, almost 80 years old, received a blow to the head, lying on the floor in a pool of blood. The young man was taken from her home and forced to ignore her. Put in the truck, when he looked up he saw before him the arrogant Genaro Sacripanti.

«You too?» he asked doubly surprised.

«It's war, you idiot,» replied that one, turning his back on him.

They were taken to a place near the castle of the Silveri Counts, located on a hill about 40 km from the village, on the edge of the plain and across the Erbio River. The castle, uninhabited for a decade, was occupied by the S.S., being there one of its commands.

Destripado was the most feared man by the inhabitants of Terracotta. Nobody knew the origin of that nickname, being his real name Alcibiades Tablet. A wicked and crafty monster, rejected by the whole community that had always denied him the slightest friendly exchange. Pimp and treacherous, capable of giving in exchange for his own profit even his own mother. To all these qualities add that of a thief. His physique made him more repugnant, hunchbacked and lame on one leg, one-eyed, with a huge nose resembling a large potato. His lip, the cause of a nervous tic, always showed the wink of a sarcastic smile. According to the evil tongues that abound in small towns, the individual even practiced witchcraft.

His fame soon reached the ear of Lieutenant Müller. Indeed, the Nazi sent for him and, after a brief interview, assigned him to an office in the town hall. His task from then on was only to provide any kind of information concerning everything that was going on in the village. In particular, he was to report on the secret activities and meetings held by the few remaining inhabitants. A very *sui generis* assignment for the bastard, who, protected by the S.S., would from that moment on commit any kind of felony.

Destripado was also aware of the romance between Fiorella and Simone, a fact that, although it made him happy, he considered that he was a poor young man. The proud Genaro Sacripanti had never been a saint of his devotion, but neither was he unaware of the lieutenant's intentions with regard to the young woman. He had heard her mentioned with particular interest one afternoon while the officer was having tea at Ru's house, a famous prostitute, protected by high-ranking Nazi officers. It is obvious to say that Fiorella's beauty was known by all the inhabitants of the entire region.

The infamous Ripper, in order to ingratiate himself with Müller, was quick to inform him where he could find her. «*Herr* Lieutenant, I know where you can find Fiorella Sacripanti. The Perpetual Father usually meets every evening.»

9

# THE POLITICIAN OF CURUCUCÚ

The leader received a standing ovation, especially from María's daughters. An auspicious closing of campaign for the first time that seasoned politician felt in the adhesion of the people the sure and spontaneous support. a community once apathetic, rather hostile, had become beautiful and ready to give its support.

A suspicious man, he promised that, through him, justice would act swiftly and firmly. The heinous crime of Don Getulio would not go unpunished. The inhabitants of Curucucú should trust him and his promises. He would also intervene before the archbishopric of first and soon they would have a new shepherd of souls. Police protection would soon be a reality.

«I swear before all of you and on the bones of my ancestors that rest under this ground, that the murderers of Don Getulio will go to jail. The entire people of Curucucú will henceforth be able to live and work in peace, protected and protected by the laws and justice. I will be a full-time defender of your rights. Mine will be the commitment to help the dispossessed, the forgotten, the marginalized. From my seat where you installed me with your votes, my heart and my efforts will always be directed towards Curucucú».

The crowd, won over by the avalanche of promises, applauded thunderously. Even the sheep at the end of Calle Real were lying on the sidewalks, ruminating on their indolence.

«What do we do now?» asked Bagri to the mayor. «Are you still the authority and you ask?»

The questioned person shrugged his shoulders and leaned a chair against the wall, letting himself fall into it. Then spitting out a chew of *chimó*, he muttered: «The river has brought us this far».

10

# MARÍA JOSEFINA

On August 21, 1915, a rose was born. She was very pretty and the parents, when they saw her, said she looked like a little angel. She is the fifth of the siblings, who were a total of five. She grew up as a rose, pretty and cautious. Through the years she was a good student and very Catholic. She lived through the war of the 40's and married a great man, Vincenzo Di Sclafani, in 1931.

She had seven children, five girls and two boys. She was always proud of her children and as time went by, they married. Unfortunately the second daughter died at the age of 58, 20 years after being operated on for breast cancer. After 20 years she got careless, the second daughter was going to get married and she did not have the treatment. She was very ill and died, leaving her young husband with two children and three granddaughters.

A daughter died 7 years ago. She was doing very well during a vacation with the daughter and grandchildren and went to town. Several cousins came to see her and she was happy, apparently in good health. She was 85 years old when she got up from a chair and said «I feel sick». She hugged her cousin and died hugging him. The doctor was called and she was dead. Her heartbeat was dropping and with a simple pace-maker she would have been saved. All the religious services were held in the village church. Father said: «here she was baptized, here she was confirmed, here she was married and here the religious services were held». Her children took her to be buried in Torino, where she lived.

Another son died 3 years ago, a male who was 79 years old. He was left with three females and one male, eleven grandchildren, eight great-grandchildren. Having lived through a thousand calamities with the war, malaria and went to bed in the mother's house. Her husband went to war for a year and at that time there was no electricity, no water, no plumbing. She got by as best she could.

At that time, bread was made in the houses with firewood, the oven was heated, and the dough was made with the «arbitrio de ramo». There was a hole in the floor and there was a handle to turn it. It was then dried in Termine. They put a machine to make it and it came out wet. She brought it to town to dry it, but later they put in a factory that dried it in town. That was all work for her.

In 1950 she set up the loom belonging to her great-great-grandmother. She put it in her house and made several weavings. The linen cloth came out dark because the linen was dark and she had to iron it in April, in the field, next to a water trough. Before it dried she had to pour water on it. She left it white and then she divided it among all her children to embroider it, to make sheets, tablecloths with napkins, tablecloths.

As you can see, she worked hard all her life. All her children were well married to good people, but they died before she did. The first one, making a grill, threw something on it to light the fire. When it didn't light, he poured it on again. His hand got wet and caught fire. He was taken by ambulance to the hospital, in a glass room with a computer on his head. They did a lot of grafts, but none worked because he was so depressed. Eventually he died, but there were still investigations as to how that happened. They could not take him out of the hospital until the investigation was finished. That was in Italy.

The other son was a smoker and did not take his circulation pill. He was 77 years and 6 months old and died from lack of circulation in his head. The second son was going to sell a racing car and was testing it when a motorized vehicle ran into him. He drove his leg into a tree and almost got stuck in the tree. It took him a year to heal it.

As you can see, she did not have a quiet life. All the grandchildren are professionals and are her pride and joy. Her husband died of lung cancer at the age of 70 years and 6 months. She was able to celebrate her 90th birthday with a lot of partying, but was widowed at 64. The eldest daughter was widowed at 66 and the last one at 68.

As you can see, he had good things and bad things. He died at the age of 95 because his kidneys shut down, in February 2009. His remaining children all live in Italy, are great businessmen and very happy. One of them married at the age of 19 and went to Venezuela. She lived there for 55 years and moved 9 years ago to Orlando, in the United States, because the eldest son had a son.

This is definitely the story of the *Nonna*.

11

# THE DI SCLAFANI FAMILY

My father's name was Vincenzo Di Sclafani Lo Preste. I am Teresa Di Sclafani, blonde, and always close to him. My father used to tell me that writing was something I had from birth. I never had a deep study of history, but I did study in the town where I was born.

There I did not inherit a great fortune, but I did inherit the memory of belonging to an important family, descendant of Emperor Di Sclafani. A lineage that, for lack of support and loss of privileges, saw its reign vanish.

All of us who are left of that family name were forced to live with less. To work from the bottom, with effort. No Di Sclafani had ever left Italy. They all stayed there, becoming great entrepreneurs, but within the country.

I, on the other hand, did not emigrate on my own: I got married, and with my husband we went to Venezuela. My father-in-law, Antonio Nasca, did not emigrate like others; he bought a piece of land, although he never saw it.

That land was where my town is today: Alia. At that time, the school only went up to fifth grade, but before that, even in first grade, we were taught to divide and multiply.

I studied at the San Giuseppe school, an old two-story house. I remember the large classrooms, and how, when they finished that old school, they built a new, more modern one.

I have seen so many wars in the world, so many conflicts that make me think that the real prison is not only physical, but political: a prison made by the governments in power and the dictatorships that have arisen in several countries.

All this is born, unfortunately, from dark roots disguised as work and power. It also happened in countries like Italy or Spain, where the generals dominated and people were forced to work in chains, tied up, without freedom.

I remember one of those times: General Angarita, who rode a bicycle in Miraflores. They were public figures, and all the people acted with the obedience of the nuns in church.

They said that Venezuela was going to be solved, that everything would get better, but it was not so. No politician gave life to Venezuela or turned out to be a good leader. Democracy, in Venezuela, did not bear the fruits that were expected. Some who did not steal, simply did not do anything. And those who did steal, did even worse, harming everyone.

There were dictatorships that, despite their mistakes, at least protected the country to some extent. Until 2013, there was stability. But then came someone like Maduro, and everything got worse.

Difficult times were also experienced in Colombia. Politicians were singled out there, such as Carlos Andrés, a Colombian with links to the guerrillas. The children - the young people - were kidnapped in Colombia. Some were registered at the borders, others right here. And to this day, the children are still carrying all that, living the consequences, inheriting the effects of those dark times.

They built the modern school until the sixth grade was completed, in a place near my father's house. Even today, I still can't explain why I am so attracted to these stories. Our family history has been written in three books. Of those, only one has been published, and it is undoubtedly the most important, because it shows how I saw the world and what I lived as Teresa Di Sclafani.

This book has been very successful, and that makes me very happy. In its pages we talk about great figures, such as the King of Spain and the President, and also about Don Cipriano, whom I recognize as one of the first leaders of a great nation.

I remember a governor named Marco, who suffered much more than the others, because while others solved everything over the phone, he really lived it, facing situations head on. That is why I admire him: because he accumulated all the moments that really educate, and he made decisions together with important corporations.

I created a corporation, Lo Preste Blanda - my family's surnames - are part of that legacy. My grandson, who bears those names, would have a great fortune today. He buys everything on his own.

Lo Preste is a prominent surname, a branch that was a large landowner on my father's side. The Blanda family, on the other hand, was on my mother's side. Neither the Lo Preste, nor the Blanda, nor the Orfanello, nor the Todaro: none of them emigrated.

And those surnames are not excluded from my presence. I am proud to carry them inside me, because they represent an example, a living continuity. The Di Sclafani family still preserves greatness. I know it, I feel it, I affirm it. Di Sclafani comes from my ancestors. And Di Sclafani wine is still sold in Sicily and all over Italy.

The Lo Preste's were rich and didn't care about anything. I remember well what he was like in the village, even though I was only five years old at the time. He had such a strong way about him, an energy that, for me as a child, was hard to understand.

At that time, Hitler killed more than six million. Everything was blown up, millions of lives lost. People were dying everywhere, even the blood of the poorest was taken.

Orthodoxy, rituals, were used to consecrate violence in the name of the youth, of the people. Although the people had some food, the situation was constantly changing. They moved, they moved away, even in the squares. They slept under makeshift roofs, like guerrillas who never surrendered.

Then came the First World War, where my grandfather died in 1917: Gaetano Di Sclafani. And also a cousin, Vincenzo Di Sclafani, who came back without a leg, and was left in a wheelchair. I was a child, but my father took me to meet him. He told me, «This is your Uncle Vincenzo.» His hair was gray and curly.

At that time, there was always talk of a land that was in dispute between Italy and others. The war, at first, was not so bad. The Germans and the Italian government were not all bad at the time. But as time went on, they started the harsh governments that imposed compulsory military service.

People were abandoning their lands, order broke down, and everything was organized by force. As time went by, bullets, violence, and finally, death arrived.

In those days, if one fell in the hospital, the expense was paid, and that came out of taxes. Thanks to the President of that time, that situation changed for the emigrants.

Many came from other places, and with them the expenses also grew. There was a communist government which, carried with pride, made nations begin to live very well, as happened in Uruguay.

Uruguay was going through a serious system of laborism, where women, in order to take their children to school, even had to be armed. I remember when old Mujica, a 75-year-old man, arrived. He did manage to put an end to gangs. He put the name of Uruguay on high, and he did not do it out of ambition: he did not receive his full salary, and in the end he left poor, singing with his old lady, as it is told in the story.

There was also President Lula da Silva in Brazil. During his first term, he did not do things so well, but in his second term he is doing much better. That is a communist government too. And it does not matter if it is called dictator, democrat or communist: what matters is what is in their blood.

There have been dictatorships in countries like Italy, Germany and Rome. There was a lot of talk about monarchies, and how the powerful sent others to the asylum, while the simple people went on with their lives.

In those times, Italy was much better off under the monarchy system. Although it is also true that in the villages nothing arrived. There was a lack of water, electricity, sewers. The governors did nothing. They were just names, but they didn't deliver.

12

# MY GRANDCHILDREN

My grandson Enzito is a soccer player. He led his team and led them to form a great group. A very good group, as true soccer players should be, who do it for passion, to pass the time, but without neglecting their training.

Your college career will be very important. He will graduate with honors. He showed great intelligence from a very young age: he is already going to study robotics engineering, a career of the future.

From the first vote, she showed maturity to participate, to work, to function, even in the most mundane things like cooking. I know he will take care of me someday. Since he was a child, he had already registered a program in the commercial registry.

He did it with affection, as a gift for Salvatore, who has been a great student, dancer as well, and soccer player.

I am sure he will be a great businessman. Because of his friendliness and his dedication to business, he has that natural charisma. The youngest, Salvatore Antonio, has also been a soccer player since he was a child.

He trains as a karateka. He is only two ribbons short of being a black belt, like his grandfather I am very proud of my three grandchildren: they are 11, 14, and 16 years old.

Salvatore Antonio is very much like his grandfather: he runs just as he did, although in his grandfather's time there were no computers. Salvatore has won 6 trophies. He is champion in Orlando, in Milano and in Sicily. I am proud of him, and of all my grandchildren.

# 13

## UNITED STATES

In Berlin, the wall came down. The President was an actor, a career man, not just a politician. He made it in time. That wall marked an era. It made the United States have a good government.

This is part of the history of the world, of the great stories that have changed nations. El Salvador, this country full of criminals, is moving forward. The country has recognized all those criminals: they have them tied up by their arms and legs, and they have put them in small, restricted prisons, with no frills or comforts.

Proudly, the United States has not hesitated to call dangerous thieves by their name. And anything is possible, if you have the talent and the will.

The President was a socialist who died recently, at the age of 100: Jimmy Carter. He had a worldwide organization that made a lot of money. His descendants are still going to countries to fix what is left after death, what he left behind. Thanks to that, my family also got ahead. Carter's organizations helped get another president started. Still, not everyone trusted this great country. After four years, people were protesting. But he was a true democrat.

And I tell you: I am not complaining, nor am I leaving. With all the Presidents that this great country has had, most of them have been gentlemen, at the service of the people. This is a great country, and this is part of the great history of the United States of America. We will make history together with courage and unity!

**14**

# OSELLITO

The story of Osellito and Luisita is not a novel. It is a life experience, a story of men and women who face the unexpected every day.

We add our experiences to the books I write, as a cycle within my family. A family friend had two sons. One of them fell in love with a girl with whom he shared from school, through elementary school, middle school, and even high school.

Happy to have achieved everything with good grades, they both went on to college, pursuing the same career: medicine. After completing their five years of studies, they each chose their own specialty: she became a gynecologist and he a cardiologist.

Over time, he had opportunities in various medical departments. First as an internist, and later he excelled as a contributor to scientific journals. He came to be considered an eminence. His parents were proud: they had fulfilled that first stage of youth. The young people married and formed their own home. They had a little girl, who at the time of this writing is three years old.

But it wasn't all joy. Later, another woman appeared, one who pretended to be a friend of both of them. This woman was sowing discord, until she managed to separate the husband from his wife by means of witchcraft and manipulation.

The man, confused, ended up leaving the wife he loved so much. And he married that woman. That woman was called «perverse woman». Years later, she also had a daughter, who is now 12 years old. That woman, the perverse one, has dominated the house, has manipulated everything with her presence and her way of walking. The perverse one gained nothing. She was left alone and badly off, without her daughter. That is the sad end for her and the happy end for Osellito. He is very happy.

One day a dictator came and told the parents that he was going to the United States to start his own business. The mother worked hard, and sometimes went to visit her daughter on Friday nights. She would come back tired on Sunday. Now she tells me this story...

The story is that this lady, because of all the work she was doing, interrupted a pregnancy. She took two pills, and that caused the fetus -which was already formed as a hand- to break. She got so scared that she called an Uruguayan lady who had a cafeteria across the street.

The Uruguayan lady said, «Don't be scared. It is normal. That is a fetus. Another woman is going to get pregnant in Puerto Rico». So she said.

I was traveling very tired, and on two occasions Osellito appeared to me at the airport in Caracas. The first time, at the airport, when she arrived, she told him that she was tired. I answered him: «I am afraid because there were thieves». Then he took the books out of the backpack and put it under his head. He took off his dark blue suit and put it on over his head.

As time went on, the first daughters were given gifts every year. When they came back from vacation, they were given everything. But it is not enough to give things to the children: you have to give them love, every day.

The first wife, after ten years, married a good man who loved her. They are happy. When he was about 25 years old, they were presented with what they considered a miracle: his wife, who was 32 years old, became pregnant, even though she could not.

She worked non-stop, from Monday to Sunday, until very late. Her husband worked far away, 2000 kilometers away. He only came on Sunday mornings and returned in the evening.

She stayed with her children: a 10-year-old and a 4-year-old, cooking for them and cleaning the house. The children attended a Catholic school, and she continued to work.

The children grew up. The oldest, at the age of 17, was taken to the United States. There he studied for 10 years and graduated as a mechanical engineer, marketing manager, and with computer training. He then returned to his country and started working in his spare parts business, after several years...

When she was 28 years old, she went for a consultation. There he asked if what was happening to him was due to something his mother had done to him. They said, «What are you saying? That's your mother.

He was married with a daughter, but in time, another woman - a perverse one - fell in love with him. She did a lot of witchcraft on him until he divorced her so he could marry the wicked one. Fourteen years passed without him realizing that he was under witchcraft.

It was the mother of the miracle - the same one who had experienced something similar - who, seeing the envy that this perverse woman had for them, realized that they had done witchcraft to her. So they sent her for a spiritual «check-up».

While she was already in the process of divorce, the perverse one did another witchcraft even stronger, and also against the mother of the miracle. Nobody noticed this until it was too late. Thus the circle was closed: the river of wickedness had swept everyone away.

Evil exists. There are brutalities that some women commit without any scruples. That is why we must beware of bad women. I wrote this page for the men of today. To serve as a guide, as a warning against those women without heart or conscience. Because a man, when he is noble, should never dare to do the same wickedness.

She, who was always cold, covered herself with everything she could. At eight o'clock in the morning the plane was leaving for her transfer. At that time she called her mother: «Mommy, mommy, the plane is about to leave,» she said. She replied: «My angel, may the angels watch over you». They did not see each other. He told her he didn't know anything.

Again in the closed airport in Caracas, at dawn the rats were coming out and she was afraid of them. He looked for a couch, a chair, and made her lie down. «We control the rats,» he told her. At 8 am he called her again and told her that his plane was leaving for Barquisimeto.

For six years he had needed a cardiologist. He asked her to help him find one. The son recommended one: there was a cardiologist with a good CV at a hospital downtown. They liked the doctor. Then he came to Osceola Hospital.

The lady, who visited them frequently, one day pointed out to them a picture hanging on the wall, with a carved wooden frame, and underneath it read the name of Professor Osellito. That day, at the end, the doctor told her: «It was not you, it was his spirit. He who came with you in time, that spirit brought much more affection».

An elderly Puerto Rican man told him: «I am very studious about incarnations. Do the DNA tests». She had them done on May 20 and on the 28th she went for a consultation. He asked her if she had been tested and she replied that she knew she was his mother. The miracle of the baptism godmother, sister of the mother, was born sick at heart. She died on her 11th birthday and put her in all the church theaters. He took her everywhere.

She would go to mass in the morning and then start sewing. One day her mother's sister died, a girl who had a malfunction, and her mother went to accompany her sister, because her husband was in Venezuela. A disaster in the family. She was left alone with the niece and cried, saying that if she died, she would be left alone.

The miracle of 74 years ago, there was no doctor specialized in cardiology in the village. He wanted to leave a cardiologist in the family. Full resemblance, minus the eyes and forehead. Intelligent, hardworking, submissive and helpful. He got all that from the mother of the miracle.

# 15

## THE SOLDIERS

Great is my homeland Venezuela! It was made great by the subordinates, those who obey, those who fight.

My general attends to them. «I have a high fever,» I told him, «I'm going to rest, I'm sick.» And he replied, «You don't work on the orders of a subordinate.» That's how the «Mattonfa» operation was stopped for a few days.

During that time I was taken to México. There they locked me up, and there I met a great friend who helped me to get out. One day a young man arrived, very polite, handsome, very sweet and fine, and I will never forget him. It was Mr. Amedeo, who helped me to get out of that prison in hiding. He visited me and told me that my cause was lost, but that he would help me to solve it. And so it was.

Whenever you turn everything around, it is because there are those who do not give up. My colonel was doing very well. My general, on the other hand, was bored: «There is nothing anymore,» he said. «Your affairs will be settled with my permissions,» and he authorized the colonel to act.

Then the colonel, together with a group of subordinates, organized everything and made it ready. My general told us: «We will go to the nearby cities. We will leave Calvillo at five o'clock».

We went. And from there I left for the United States. Mr. Amedeo was not to blame for anything. Just as «Caballo» is called, so was the struggle: direct, without revolutions, but with force.

We finished this mission. One of the sons did not want to testify. But you know: he who retires without having fought will never be a good soldier. And this general was a great man. He will be remembered with respect. Because life, sometimes, is very false. It is mean. It shapes men and women harshly.

Amidst the patriotic fervor, a voice resounds with determination: «I am like a Garibaldi, a Napoleon in my country. I am willing to give my life for this land I love.»

Excitement takes hold of those present. They applaud loudly. He turns to his general - Gnidasi - who firmly supports him. He even encourages him to take the photos, to load the horses and join the farmers further away, far from the political hubbub.

And here comes the reflection: the political world is not what it seems. There are capable politicians, but we need someone truly prepared, someone who knows how to lead the Republic on the right path.

The general tells him clearly:

«We must stay away from revolutions.»

«Let's get on with the evolution.»

«We need a good President.»

Others respond with loyalty:

«We are with you.»

«We have friends like you.»

«We would like you to be President!»

Someone evokes Pancho Villa.

«We'd all like to have a leader like that.»

In the midst of this environment, a young woman suddenly approaches. With her energy, she awakens an impulse of surprise. Something falls - a cup, an object - and someone exclaims, «What a beautiful and brave girl!»

She apologizes. He, with nobility, answers her:

«Don't worry. I'll do something.»

«I will obey them.»

The scene closes with a reflection: they are waiting for the general. It is the anguish that kills, not the work.

There are those who remember that even the women who loved Pancho Villa followed him faithfully, took him into their homes. And at that moment, the rumor appears that the man has a friend who supports him, who loves him, and who, if necessary, will be ready to defend him... with all her artillery.

# 16

# PERVERSE WOMEN

Women who try to remain single often do so out of habit, and sometimes out of vice. The men on duty have fun with them, they look for them at night, they look at them, they touch them, and they say things to them while they watch them. They already know what they are going to, because many of them already have many boyfriends, and they always have one «in reserve».

This is how it goes: they dress up, they dress provocatively, they wear hats, work clothes, as if they were independent, but in reality they do it to cover what they don't want to show.

Every day they dress up with stuffed animals, or distract themselves by playing with different dolls, because they have a whole series: they paint their eyes, they protect themselves with masks, they put on make-up with bright paints.

They drink very strong drinks, so as not to eat, so as not to sleep with just anyone every night. But for them, all this is a source of pride, they feel «rich», even if their wealth is only the money they take from men.

They always carry a little dog, which accompanies them in a luxurious car. They look like rich ladies, although they are not: it is only money they have taken from men who invite them to fancy restaurants and luxury hotels.

They get them drunk and then take advantage of them. No one realizes it, neither they themselves, nor their mothers, nor anyone around them. They are proud of this way of life, a life that their own mothers have already lived, that's why... this case seems more like a fairy tale, but told in reverse.

I, as an older and experienced woman, firmly believe that wicked women do the most harm. Man, by nature, is calm. When he loves, he really loves. He believes that his home is untouchable, he believes that no one could destroy it. While he thinks positively, how to make his family grow, she - the perverse woman - thinks how to destroy all that easily, sowing discord among all her own.

This woman manages to gain the trust of all the members of the family, and with that she makes their lives impossible. She is at home every day, eating, drinking, spending what little money there is, even when she doesn't need it.

And so, little by little, those who have nothing end up on the street, while she achieves her purpose: she has a house, a daughter, she no longer needs a husband, nor is she interested in him. She leaves him and gets divorced. This is the sad story of a man who has only fallen in love.

17

# THE SINGER

Today's young people are joyful: they dance, they sing, they enjoy with enthusiasm. For them, that is true happiness.

A man gets on stage, he is a well-known singer, very successful, and he keeps singing so loud that even the floor moves. During his show, he shouts to another: «Hey, give me my money, I'm going to sing here every day!» And everyone laughs.

Then he says proudly: «They have to know that I can sing.» The young people cheer up. When he sings a song for the youth, the dancers follow his steps, and the audience, in chorus, accompanies him. The ovations, the flowers they throw him, the looks he receives? all that makes a singer fall in love with a girl.

And this time, he really falls in love. He is very much in love. She, with irony, tells him: «Marry a nurse better, a sanguine like you, but not me». And yet, when he sings with emotion, she can't help but listen to him, even though she pretends not to be interested.

He plans to travel, to get away. He doesn't like big cities, he prefers the village. Young people travel with a suitcase, a hat, knock on doors where they will stay.

She asks, «Does Mr. Antonio Alto live here?».

«Yes,» they reply. «Come in, miss.»

«What a surprise!» he exclaims. «I congratulate you on your performances!»

That night, Joseph arrives, and says with joy: «I am Joseph», and someone said to him: «I'm Pepe ».

«First you, you don't remember yourself, Antonio. You were very rude. I went to see him today, and there he was, singing, distracted, paying no attention. He says he's in the field, and you're here too, doing your thing. I didn't tell you that you were at the ranch, Antonio...»

It's not possible for you to get like that, to react like it doesn't matter. You can't use your business for that. Well... I'm telling you secretly: I'm going to try something. Another young woman showed up.

But he didn't like the sergeant. He told the boys:

«Because of you, I lost her.»

«The songs were for her.»

But she pretends to be important, as if she doesn't like the *ranchero*. She treats him like he's worthless. As if she doesn't care.

«If he wants me, let him look for me» -she says and in the meantime, she makes everyone nervous.

A lady tells him, «I don't have time to attend to him.»

Antonio, who was the first -the referent, the favorite- now does not show himself. And until I tell, no one will know.

I'm not going to stay with him. I love him, yes... but he loves you. And I see myself sitting, yes, on a bench, next to him. What can I say?

Antonio did not attend to me. He is haughty. That Antonio - the first one- has land, a lot of work in the fields. He can't do anything else. But he lives very well on his ranch. And she... she goes with him.

18

# THE SCHOOL TEACHER

The person we are talking about here grew up in a good and hard-working family. He had a mother and father who always thought of their children, giving them the most important thing: education. This education was forged within the home, with solid values that gave the protagonist a good personal foundation.

For this reason, today he is recognized as a good person. His family, although humble, was distinguished by its commitment to work and effort. In that environment, it was instilled in all of them, both men and women, that they should learn to fend for themselves. The teaching was clear: well-being comes from work. And if there are difficult moments, if one does not feel happy, the only valid response is to move forward with dignity and courage.

In San Miguel de Los Altos lived a young unemployed woman who was eager to improve herself. One day she was offered a position as a teacher in a small school located in a remote hamlet. To get there, she had to cross vast plains and mountains for several days. Finally, she arrived in San Antonio de Los Altos, where she was kindly welcomed by a peasant director who took her to the school: a humble country hut.

The school lacked resources, but it was the only place of learning for children of different ages. The young girl had to teach them all together, each with their own needs. This demanded so much of her voice that she ended up almost deaf. However, her patience was admirable. She managed to get a small house to live in, in the home of an old woman who shared the home with her children. In return, she was offered food every morning and evening.

Eventually, a young man from the village fell in love with her. Although she resisted at first, she eventually accepted his affection. This young man was the only one who really stayed close to her. His family was well off, but there was no telephone in the hamlet, so everything had to be communicated by letter. Replies were slow in coming, but she was not impatient.

She was happy with her work and grateful to have been sent there. The hamlet had its church, its priest, a sacristan, and she devoutly attended mass before the start of each day. The children respected her and asked about her: the teacher who brought light into their lives.

# ON THE RADIO

Teresa Di Sclafani De Nasca's books are featured on *CapicúaFM* radio, which is heard all over planet Earth on CapicúaFM via CapicúaFM.com and leading podcasting applications.

# ABOUT THE AUTHOR

Teresa Di Sclafani De Nasca was born in Italy. She has also lived in Venezuela and the United States.

# OTHER WORKS BY TERESA DI SCLAFANI DE NASCA

- *The world according to Teresa Di Sclafani*

- *Diary of Teresa Di Sclafani*

- *The Mafia according to Teresa Di Sclafani*

- *Nonna's Stories - I*

Each is available in Castilian, English and Italian.

www.ingramcontent.com/pod-product-compliance
Lightning Source LLC
Chambersburg PA
CBHW042033120726
47911CB00026B/722